Love Lost and Truth Found – Volume 1

Sherrie Tennessee

CONFESSION

There comes a point when you finally have to be good enough for you
~ Panache Desai.

CONTENTS

PART 1 – LOVE LOST

Lost in Love

I would be lying if I said it was all bad, there was plenty of good, which is why it was so hard to leave. You taught me to stand true to who I am in our relationship. In the past, I would lose myself in love, becoming a reflection of the man in my bed, hoping to become his everything and making him mine. I lost me in love. I thank you for forcing me to keep myself and my life in our time together. You wouldn't allow me to be swallowed whole in your world. And you never fully saw mine so there was no way to lose yourself in it. My truth was found, I am enough just as I am. In that realization, I lost the lies of love and true love—self-love was found.

Outside Looking In

I always saw you as a monster here to hurt me. It wasn't until I stepped back and saw the entire picture that I saw you protected me. You held me in your mouth between your teeth, never crushing me but hiding me from those who had actually come to destroy me. I hated you for so long, caging me inside of you. I can finally thank you for keeping me safe in the last place anyone would look.

Arm's Distance
You have kept me at arm's distance.
Pulling me in but never into your heart, only to push me further away.
You have pushed me so far away that my only choice is to walk away.

Two Wrongs Don't Equal a Right
You did me wrong, it was never quite right. You showed me who you were, and it took me a while to believe. Still, the hardest step was walking away from you and back towards me.

Dead Pieces
There is a piece of your heart I will never have. It doesn't belong to another for it is dead. Years of neglect and mistreatment have led to necrosis of your heart. Do I stay and try to bring life back to it or do I walk knowing it's not my battle to fight?

I Never Had a Chance
You feed me the same lies you told the rest.
The walls were high, but I was willing to climb.
You loved to see how many hoops I would jump through to get to your heart
as you toyed with mine.
Dangling the hopes of true love and happily ever after.
I never saw the black hole that was your heart until it swallowed me whole.

The Lies Told
He entered me as a friend
He is deep inside and tells me he loves me
From behind he asked me to be his wife
With me on top, he tells me he is never going to let me go
My heart and soul were open to being loved—only to never see him again

My Turn

I stood in my place as the maid of honor, tears rolling down my face. To the outside world, they were tears of joy, only I knew the difference. I had been holding them for years and couldn't hide the hurt any longer; I could finally release the pain and move forward with my life. I was moving 3000 miles away in the morning and that, too, was my secret. I needed to get as far away as possible and start afresh.

Let me backtrack; the wedding was a joyous occasion. It was the union of my older sister Dede to her prince charming Danny. Dede, short for Diandra, was born three years before me and she was perfect – literally. With a black mother and white father, she was the definition of exotic; 5'3, 120 lb. and curves in all the right places. Dede was more than just a pretty face, she had brains too. She was valedictorian of her class, a pre-med major with a full-scholarship at Vanderbilt University in Nashville, TN.

I, on the other hand, was the middle child, Ester, 5'10, 210lb, a true brick house with a head full of kinky, curly, unruly hair. I barely made it out of high school, which was a surprise to my teachers and parents who had the same expectations for me as Dede. I was clueless as to what I was going to do with my life; I simply had to trust the process. There were quite a few stops on the road to my purpose in life, which was a very different story for both of my siblings.

My younger brother, Frank, was the baby boy and the apple of my father's eye. He had a ball in his hand since he came out the womb and was a star athlete—quarterback, point guard, and pitcher. He was an OK student, but that didn't matter, he was going to get a scholarship to the school of his picking with plans of becoming a pro in any sport he wanted and that could mean more than one. He was really that good.

My parents did their best to love us all equally; they shared a love of learning, naming us in alphabetical order. Celestine was their first born, she died shortly after birth. So my parents never took us for granted and encouraged us to find our greatness. Dede and Frank were blessed to find theirs early; mine would take a little longer. I did what I could to find my place in the world including a stint on the girls' high school basketball team. I was tall enough to be a star the coach said; sadly, I didn't have the coordination or skills to match my height. I averaged 20 seconds a game and only if we were winning by 20 points. I didn't have the brains of my sister or the athleticism of my brother, I felt like the meat between two pieces of (wonderful) bread. My family encouraged me to explore my options, from court clerk to medical assistant, it felt like I was going to have to go to the end of the earth to find my place. All that changed the day I walked into Beyond Beauty Salon. It was a new place in town, that focused on natural hair. Dede had been blessed with waist long, long, wavy, jet-black hair. I, on the other hand, got the kinky, curly afro that reached for the sky more than my back. Years of perms, coloring, texturizing, and curling to get the good hair look had left my hair fried and in need of repair. Beyond Beauty was a solace, with women in the chairs and on the walls who embraced their natural locks.

The shop was actually owned by a friend from high school, Denise. Her family had an entrepreneurial spirit, her father Mr. Davis owned several restaurants including a McDonald's and Popeyes. They also owned a cleaners, which Mrs. Davis ran. Denise and her brother Danny owned the shop; she had attended cosmetology school and he was a barber.

Danny and a friend from barber school did haircuts on one side while Denise styled natural looks for both ladies and men. It was a great concept that was successful from the first day they opened the doors. I was blown away by the experience and asked Denise how I could become a part of the team. I had more time than money and a real desire to do something new. So, I started at the bottom as the shampoo girl, it was a big title for the cleaning lady. I swept up the hair, restocked the towels, and cleaned the sinks and toilets. It was a great learning opportunity and I absorbed everything like a sponge. The more comfortable I became with the staff and clients the easier it was for me to come out of my shell. It's funny, I had known Denise and Daniel for years, we had gone to school together. Danny was two years older than me; he was always nice, clean cut, with the best high-top fades in school. Danny saw my passion and desire to learn, so he took me under his wing. He taught me the business side of the industry—how many clients you need a day, week, month, a year to truly turn a profit. He explained the ebbs and flow of the industry; you must plan for September and January, the typically slowest months of the year. He talked about the flow of the location, marketing, and how to keep clients coming back again and again. He was a savvy business owner, a good friend and the best mentor I could have ever asked for and helped me step into myself. After two years of apprenticing, with countless early mornings and late nights, I received the title of stylist. I had studied and passed the state boards and was given my own chair and clients. I had regular customers who loved the work I did and happily spread the word.

Fast forward four years, it was Christmas season, my favorite time of year. I love the lights, sounds, and smells of the holiday. It is also one of the busiest times of year for the salon. I had been booked for weeks; I finally had my own money, a beautiful place, and finally felt like I had found my greatness. The last piece was a man to share the joy and I had my eye on one. Danny and I had become close friends, we spent a great deal of time together at the shop, traveling to attend hair shows, and planning what was next. There were plans to upgrade to the current location and thoughts of a second location. I had truly become a part of the family, so much so that I attended the annual Davis holiday party. It was a big deal and the most coveted ticket in town. I wanted to be available to talk to Danny, so another guy wasn't an option for a date. It just so happened that Dede was home on winter break, but her boyfriend was doing his residency and had to work. I had her all to myself. She would be my date to the party this year. I had it planned to the last detail; I had the perfect dress. Since my overeating to cushion the pain of failure had stopped, the extra pounds had fallen off like leaves in the fall. I was down to 180 lbs., so the form-fitting red sequence dress fit in all the right places. As a stylist, every hair on my head was in place and my makeup was flawless, skills I had picked up at the salon. I was ready to declare my love for Daniel tonight and start the new year together as a couple.

Dede and I were the hottest women at the soiree; I was excited to introduce her to my best friend, mentor and hopefully my future husband. The party lived up to expectations with a DJ, live band, full-catered spread, and Christmas swag bags that were the toast of the town. It was a magical night and I was eager to find Danny and show him off to Dede. I had finally won—or so I thought. As soon as I saw Danny, I waved him over to meet Dede. She didn't remember Danny from high school, she was an upperclassman who was courted by the biggest and the brightest, he didn't make it on her radar back then. Tonight, he was decked out in a black suit and red bow tie, smelling good, looking great with a smile bright enough to light the sky. There was something different about him tonight; I would come to understand why later.

Dede was her kind, sweet self and this is why I love her. She is genuinely a good person. The introduction was simple and perfectly timed as I was called away to meet with vendors. I had developed my own line of natural hair products over the past two years. My clients and Danny encouraged me to take it to the next level. I worked the room while Dede and Danny caught up. She was in medical school getting ready to start her residency; she was dating a fellow student a few years older than her. Danny talked about the shop, how things were going and how proud he was of me. The two people I wanted to impress most in the world were talking about how great I was. It was a dream come true. Once I was able to make my rounds, Dede and I kept Danny on the dance floor the rest of the night. We laughed, talked, and reminisced about times gone by; it would be a night to remember. I never had the chance to talk to Danny about my feelings. There never seemed to be a right time, I was so wrapped up in the upcoming projects and I didn't want the conversation to feel forced. I didn't understand until much later what had actually happened that night.

There was a sparkle in Danny's eyes I had never seen before, and, of course, in my naivety, I thought it was me or the fact that he had just signed on a celebrity client to the location. Actually, Danny didn't just remember Dede; she was his secret crush in middle and high school, Dede being the person she was, always friendly and smiling at everyone including Danny. It was the highlight of his day to see her smile and he swore that one day he would make her smile. He never forgot how special she had made him feel and he was determined to keep his promise in returning the favor. It wasn't until that night that he realized that Dede was my sister, partly because I never talked about my family at work. I focused on my craft and becoming the best, probably because I never felt good enough in my own house.

We all hung out during the holiday break with Dede coming by the shop to see all the changes and, of course, to get a new look for the new year. The time flew, and Dede was back in school and I was focused now more than ever on launching the product line. I was arranging my travel calendar to hit as many of the hair shows as I could to speak and promote the line. Danny, it seemed, was focused on the expansion plans. He would occasionally ask me how Dede was doing in passing, just small talk. At the same time, Dede had decided to end the relationship with her boyfriend to focus more on her schooling. As fate would have it, the hair show was in Nashville, TN, not too far from Dede's school. So, I arranged for Dede, Danny and I to have dinner after the show to catch up. I didn't anticipate winning the show and being courted by national salons and product reps, vendors and the sort. I sent Danny to cheer up Dede after her breakup while I worked on becoming a brand.

It wasn't until the night before the wedding that I learned that Dede had realized over the holiday break that she wasn't happy. She had more fun with Danny than she'd had her in whole life. She ended the relationship with her doctor boyfriend to ensure she was able to explore the possibility of being with Danny. So the dinner I set up and missed was Dede and Danny's first date and their declaration of love for each other. How could I not be happy for them? I never said a word to anyone about my feelings for Danny. I had barely said it out loud to myself, truly deep down I never felt enough or worthy of an intimate relationship with Danny. It seems it was fate for them—high school memories and missed opportunities, a chance meeting and dinner all engineered by me. I was credited as cupid for the lovely couple. I was given praise and accolades by each family and from industry leaders for my own creations, yet all I truly wanted was Danny's love. He finally figured out where to open the second location—Nashville. He wanted to be closer to Dede as they planned to start their life together. I was given the opportunity to run the current location and come on board as a business partner in the company. It was what I had been working for the past six years! Yet, the thought of going into the shop and not seeing Danny, knowing he was in Tennessee with my sister, was more than I could handle.

I continue to keep my feelings close to my heart, so I chose my words carefully as I wished them a lifetime of happiness. I played the role of sister, friend, matchmaker, and bridesmaid. I knew that I needed to get as far away from this situation as I possibly could! I called one of the sales reps for the hair show; they made me a godfather offer—one I couldn't refuse. I started working on manufacturing my own product line on a global scale. It was stressful and time-consuming, just the distraction I needed as the wedding drew close. The products sold like gang-busters, reaching over a million dollars in sells in three months! The company wanted me to start traveling for the next 9 months promoting the line, speaking and training at demos at the top shows. The company was footing the bill for everything. My bags were packed, my condo was rented for the next year, and the car was coming to pick me up at 5 am for the 8 am flight. I was finally ready to get some stamps on my passport, grow into the woman I was meant to be and find a love of my own. I hadn't told a soul, I didn't want to take away from the excitement of Dede and Danny's special day. I was going to make all my dreams come true the day after. Today, I stood in support of the life and love I wanted. Tomorrow, it was my turn and I was ready for my new life.

PART 2: LOVE AND LUST

Thank You
You have loved for years stepping in and out of life
We are different each time, yet it never seems to be right
Your love has always been in the back of my heart
I thank you for loving me and who I am at every stage of my growth

Holding My Heart
I am taking my heart out of your hands and holding it in my own for that is where my true love lies.
I'm going to show you again how I love me with flowers, cards and candy but also with quality time, care, effort, consistency, kind words, laughter and dedication.
When you can show me these things, I might let you hold my heart again.

Cannabis Man
He touched me with tinctures on his tongue that took me to a high that I walked with the trees and kissed the stars, yet I never left the ground.
The high he gave me stripped me down to my core; I stood there with just the essence of me showing. He became my new drug, addicted to the freedom and the connection to the higher and wiser self.

Loving You
Somehow, in loving you, I learned to love myself more.
I let my heart be open, free from the chains of expectation and doubt.
I loved you fully and didn't need your love in return.
I walked away not knowing if you felt the same.

The Friend Zone
The drop zone, the dead and dreaded friend zone.
A place of no expectations. It's time-out in the relationship where I can wait and see.
The penalty box as a result of bad behavior.
Few start there but most end there.
It is the lack of action and misalignment of words that have placed you out of my heart and on the fringes of my life.
If you play right, maybe I'll let you back in but know you can go back to the friend zone again.

It Wasn't so Simple
I loved him most of my life
He loved me most of his
The timing never seemed quite right
There were girlfriends, boyfriends, school work, husbands, wives—life
We finally admitted it was none of those things keeping us apart
It was our fears, insecurity, and doubt then and now

Under the Stars

On a drive to a surprise destination, Chef is behind the wheel of the truck and I am playing the handy co-pilot, handling snacks, tunes, and conversation. It's been a long week, so I know he is tired. I am doing my best to keep him awake with stories, questions, and a few jokes. Chef loves to have things in his hands, so I always wear skirts for our road trips. His hand on my leg is expected anytime we get on the road. Today was different; his hand started out on my knee and then slowly moved up my thigh. With a slight moan, I let him know I was enjoying the experience. I am not sure how he was able to focus on the road and at the same time get me wet. By the time he reached my panties, my yoni was wet and eager to be explored. Slowly slipping in his middle finger in, he began to explore my pussy. Slow then fast, eager then relax, soft and rough, I couldn't hold my orgasm any longer.

He wasn't as tired as I thought. I had to return the favor of pleasure. So, with him still driving, I kissed his ears, sucked his neck, pinched his nipples, all with his smile growing bigger; I was working my way down to his treasure. Now that I have his attention I slowly unzip his pants. Chef didn't wear underwear for this trip, I see he had plans. I slip out his dick; with kisses make it jump and stand at attention. I love the sounds Chef makes when I begin to suck his dick. His accent is strong in the moment of pleasure. Slurping, sucking, licking, caressing, his dick, my goal isn't to make him cum yet. I want him inside of me. The feeling was mutual as he pulled over into secluded area. I proceeded to lift up my skirt and move my panties out of the way to make room for the deliciousness that is his dick. Starting out slow, she was wet, but it was still a little tight to get it in, that sense of pain and pleasure. Up and down, round and round, it feels so good. This was just a quickie to wake him up for that night; he had plans—mattress in the bed of the truck, he fed and fucked under the stars. Oh, my favorite Chef.

PART 3: TRUTH FOUND

Open to Love Again

I have to be open to love again. I can't sit back in the shadows with my heart tucked away, afraid to love or be hurt again.

That's not loving; it's fearing. That is not what God intended for me. We are here as a spirit being having a human experience to be loved and give love. It is the only answer and reason. Not loving is fearing and fear is death.

So I have to love again, I am not ready to die.

Living My Life

I stopped putting my life on hold until you arrive.

I love myself fully

I walk my path

I look forward to meeting you on the road to a better me

We Made, and I Raise

Our son was made in the purest love and joy of our relationship. Maybe his birth took that from our marriage. I stand here knowing the best thing that happened to me was you as you gave me the greatest gift—him. Though my ego tries to hate you, I find gratitude in the mundane moments of motherhood. I know we can never go back to that space, I do wish you stood by us as I raise your seed.

The Stew Is Brewing

Stew and Cher met through a mutual friend who saw the hurt and need for love in each of them. She knew it was a match. The meeting lacked a spark and seemed to be headed for the friendship dead zone. Then, one night, Stew was sick, and Cher made some of her soul-warming chicken soup to take to her new friend, expecting him to look like ET, wrapped in a blanket standing over a pot of water. Instead what she saw was a man willing to be seen in a vulnerable state. It was so unexpected and refreshing that her porcupine quills retracted a little. What was supposed to be a 15-minute visit turned into an all-night evening of laughter and conversation and ended with one of the most amazing kisses she'd ever had in her life. She would never tell anyone, but she felt she had been struck by lightning. Stew was very wary of dating, love, and human interaction and was also taken aback by the chemistry. The game was on, but it was a very different one than either was used to playing.

Three years without a social or love life, Stewart dedicated his life to kids. He was still recovering from a devastating breakup with his wife. His one goal since the age of twelve, when his father left, was to become exactly that—a real father. He was raised in the knowledge that babies could be made and forgotten in a weekend. It was the mother's responsibility to care for and nurture the children. He had felt the results personally and knew different. He wanted to have a successful career and be married before he brought kids into the world. This is what he did, but the perfect wife didn't create the perfect life even with two beautiful kids. He rarely discussed what was wrong, even after all these years. He stuffed that story down deep with the hurt of his father leaving.

Cherry —Cher-Cher—for short, her mother named her that after her cherry-red and perfectly-shaped lips. She had lost her cherry young and feared love and vulnerability. Cher-Cher gave her sexuality away to get attention and fill a void that never seemed to be full. She moved from place to place and man to man, never staying long enough to make anything home. Cher-Cher's career had been her saving grace and guide post amid all the other changes in her life. The kitchen was her solace and years of cooking away her heartache were finally paying off.

After five years of being single to focus on her own growth, Cher had finally learned to lead with sensuality instead of sexuality, discovering that a phone call, a mentally stimulating conversation, and creating a life she loved was more important that a night of passion. Stew was going to be her test model. She would flirt and play but not love them and leave them as she had in the past.

For the first time ever, Cher-Cher wasn't afraid to get caught in the trap of love. Just as Stew had been so vulnerable and open that night of laughter, Cher too would have to show her softer side, letting down her walls.

Stew came with his own hurt —his wife found it fit to sleep with any man that caught her eye. She was the breadwinner and traveled extensively for her job. She willed her power and commanded a presence and the attention of every man in the room. Stew was drawn to her strength, not realizing it would one day crush him. After 6 years and countless affairs, he licked his wounds, gathered what was left of his pride and walked away with a small fortune for all his pain and suffering. It would never make up for the distrust he had for women. That would take years to heal. One thing that made the situation bearable was the two beautiful kids that came from the marriage. Since his ex-wife was constantly on the road, Stew had become the primary caregiver—a stay-at-home dad.

The kids had never seen Stew with anyone but their mother at ages 7 and 10; it was a delicate matter that he wasn't sure how to navigate. It was a combination of the kids and the destruction of his marriage that led to his love drought.

Then entered Cher-Cher, she always smelled like vanilla, it must have come from all the wonderful cooking she did. That night of enlightened conversation changed him in a way he didn't think was possible. For the first time in 15 years Stew was open to the idea of falling in love again. Their friendship and ultimate courtship was different from the typical format. Both in their 40s, the need to party and hang out had long since passed. They were both responsible for others; Stew had his kids and Cher-Cher her investors.

Cher-Cher had a successful bakery 6 blocks from her condo. She had lived in and above the location for years to be close by and to save money. Now with a second location in the works and negotiations to have her goodies in a large chain store, her life had come full circle. She had always been successful in business; it was love that proved to be the challenge. Her strong personality attracted two types of men; those that were as strong as her but mostly selfish and others who wanted to be taken care of by her. Cher-Cher had time for neither. After her failed marriage, she had written off love, packed up her heart and idea of a real relationship and put the idea in a box in the back of her very full closet. She had married for love and thought it could conquer all of the faults in the relationship with her ex-husband, a chef.

It had seemed like a match made in heaven, their love of the kitchen and all things food. The sex was pretty amazing, which was the cherry on top. When they met, her husband was the executive chef at one of the top restaurants in the city. He had dreams of owning his own location, as she did. The difference was Cher-Cher was willing to do whatever it took to make it happen, even if that meant working for someone else during the day so she could bake at night. As she became more successful and her husband's dreams stalled, his resentment grew. It took two years of verbal abuse and cheating before Cher-Cher finally found the courage and strength to walk away, never looking back. Feeling devastated and defeated by love and the idea of marriage, she threw herself into making the bakery world-renowned.

That was five long years ago; since then Cher-Cher traveled and lived aboard, all the while learning and mastering a variety of baking skills that were put to use at her DC location. So, when she met Stew, love was not a goal. He was a really nice guy—friend material. She could call one of her guy friends for company, conversation, dinner, a game or museum tour. There wasn't any pressure, just a fun time had by both and that is what she had come to expect. The dating scene had changed and not necessarily for the better, everyone seemed to have a starting five lineup and sex was the criteria for dating. It was too much to handle, so Cher-Cher sat on the sidelines. She enjoyed the stories of her friends and worked on herself as well as her business. The instant chemistry was unexpected; she knew from her friend that he wasn't dating anyone else.

The romance blossomed slowly, dates, dinners, drives, and lots of laughter, which led to friendship and ultimately to a real relationship. Stew was very protective of his kids and private life. His wife was still trying to make her way back into his bed. So it was an only after a year of dating that he allowed Cher-Cher to meet his kids. At their first meeting, Cher-Cher gave them a baking lesson and completely won them over with her knowledge, passion and, of course, good tasting food. Cher-Cher enjoyed the family time with Stew and the kids; there were outings, events, dinners, and activities that filled his calendar. Cher-Cher did her best to attend what she could. Her schedule was fuller than ever and there were talks about a show on the Food Network. Stew loved his alone time with her when the kids were with their mother or grandparents. Cher-Cher's house was filled with items from her travels around the world; masks, plates, elephants, books. It was a touchable museum in the condo; like her, it always smelled of something sweet and delicious. Stew's love allowed Cher-Cher to lower her walls and remove the barbed wire that surrounded her heart for so many years. Her kind ways and trusting heart allowed Stew to open up again as well. He felt love for the first time and wanted to stay in that place forever. Though he never made her see stars in the bedroom, his tenderness and openness made up for anything that was missing.

So, after three years of dating, traveling, and intertwining their lives, the next chapter was, of course, marriage. Though it wasn't a simple as that; the kids loved their school and had finally adjusted to being shuttled between two parents, so moving wasn't an option for Stew. Cher-Cher had the same challenge with two bakeries; her wares were selling across the US, and there was the impending launch of her new baking show. The idea of moving out of her sanctuary wasn't top on her list. Stew and Cher-Cher did what they always did, made it work for them. Each kept their place; Cher-Cher had clothes, baking items, and art at Stew's place. She would stay for a few days a month. Stew had a mini-wardrobe at Cher-Cher's place for long weekends and quick getaways. It was the best of both worlds, a true win-win; both were able to stand in love and stay true to themselves and each other living the life of their dreams.

Inside Out

He loved my flaws and trauma
He loved my smart mouth and brilliant ways
He took the time to get to know me—breaking through my many walls
Most men loved me from the outside in only seeing the tough exterior
He loved me from the inside out, seeing what very few could
He allowed me to be soft and vulnerable
He loved me fully

I Love You Already

I don't know your name, but I know how you feel
I know you will love me different than anyone else
I know you will fill my life with things I didn't even know were missing
I know you have been waiting for me to get ready, I finally am
I have loved you already, but you loved me first

Now You Know – Truth Told
When action and word match, it equals alignment.
When action and words don't match, it equals struggle.
Knowing and doing are two different things.
Time and actions reveal all things.

Real Love
I am loved
I have always been
I have always been enough
I am worthy of love
I have always been beautiful—inside and out
I am whole and complete
I forgive myself
I approve of myself
I finally put self-love first
I found real love in finally loving me

Power of Words

People throw words around like leaves with no regard for where they go or what they do, not understanding that your word is your bond, making promises they never planned to keep. We follow those words like blinded sheep only to be disappointed in the lack of promise kept; we weep thinking we have done something wrong to be lied to so easily.

Remember you call on God with the words you use. It must be known that your thoughts and words are powerful things for the words used lay the foundation for life. Have you kept the promises spoken today?

LOVE LOST AND TRUTH FOUND – VOLUME 2
(INTRO)

Lady Killer

Lisa had a look of innocence that caught the eye of most men and a few ladies. She was 5'5 and the body of a dancer. She should, she had been jazz, tap, and ballet dancing since the age of four. She had dreams of dancing full time for as long as she could remember. She did music videos, backup dancing and even a few shows before her right knee gave out and ended her professional dance career. She still kept in shape doing the thing she had loved for so long, though over the years her thick thighs had grown stronger from a new step she was now known for—stomping. Only a select few knew the other side of Lisa—a killer.

On the street, the name Stomp struck fear in the heart of everyone who heard it, for the name said it all. Many would have been shocked to know that Stomp was not only a woman but a real stunner. Lisa now used her good looks and dance moves to get close to her target. Though she used many methods to take out a target, stomping was her signature move. She kept her work life totally separate from everyone except those who knew where to look and had the money to pay top dollar for the services she offered.

Lisa was wary of dating and you never knew when the man in your bed could be next on her hit list. She loved the bad boys; they were just fun and exciting and were the first to give her a glimpse into the life. She was good girl, from a very affluent family; she went to the best schools, had a new car every two years, and lived a life of luxury. Needless to say, she was bored and wanted a little adventure. Her first real boyfriend outside her social circle was one of the biggest street dealers in town. She loved hearing the stories of action on the street, who got arrested, who beat and bagged. One fateful day, she was out with her beau and was approached by a group guy from a rival crew who wanted to prove their worth. With a black belt in karate she had the ability to stand and kick most men directly in the throat, thus bringing them to their knees. Her friend was truly impressed by her ability to not only stand up for herself also put fear into men twice her size. He needed someone like her; no one would ever expect to see her coming. Her diva demeanor was the perfect cover for a lady killer.

Lisa had been able to keep her side profession a secret for almost 3 years. Her then boy toy had moved up the ranks to control the city – everything coming in and out. Though they had stopped dating, their professional relationship remained. He was her best but not her only client. There were disgruntled lovers, wives wanting revenge, husbands not wanting to deal with child support and alimony. There were those abused as youth seeking justice.

Lisa was particular in the cases she took. She had gone to school and gotten her undergrad and graduate degree in biology. She was one of the top animal researchers in the field. Lisa had known since middle school she wanted to work with animals. She cut open her first fetal pig and fell in love. This is what she wanted to do for the rest of her life. It was ironic that, at work, with her ability to sacrifice animals in a smooth, painless manner, her co-workers dubbed her Dr. Death. The title was true outside of work as well. She wore the façade well.

Lisa loved spending time with family and friends, having parties, vacations, and movies. Any excuse was enough for a get-together. Her house was the hub for many of the gatherings. Her salary from both gigs allowed her to buy a six-bedroom house out in the woods; she had space for two dogs, a miniature pig, and two goats. It was an animal lover's dream. She hosted adults' and kids' birthday parties, the animals dressed up for the festivities. She had acres of land with her neighbors' cows and horses stopping by for visits with her animals. She had a theater, a game room, a massive family room and kitchen to host the holiday family celebrations. Lisa had a sub-basement that only she could access to handle her night job. No one who ever visited her house had a clue this other section existed and that was the point. Her lives had to remain separate. On paper, Lisa had a perfect life, family and friend filled, with trips locally and abroad. She wanted for nothing, except a man to share these experiences. She wanted to settle down and start a family. That, of course, would mean giving up her stomping ways.

Lisa had seen William out at a birthday party for a friend. She had her cousin Karen, who worked for the FBI, run a full check on him, background, credit, she was even able to get a hold of the cup he was drinking out of to get a DNA sample. She had to be sure before inviting him into her life that he was clean and trustworthy, at least on the surface. She would get to know him standing up first to see if he would make it to her bedroom.

William had noticed Lisa at the party as well. It was hard not to, she floated around the room interacting with everyone at the event. She was effortless in her conversation; she was poised, confident, and almost radiant in her presence. William had heard she was a scientist for a pharmaceutical company; she was mean with a scalpel and could almost kick anyone's ass with her black belt. She was a different kind of woman and he wanted to know her better.

Assuming that she was approached on a regular basis, William decided to take things slow. He truly wanted to get to know her as a person. In this age of text messages and tweets, he called her every day to hear her voice and check how she was doing. He knew there was competition to have a spot in Lisa's life and he knew a gentleman would stand out from the crowd. William was pretty well sought after as well; he was the Senior Vice President of Marketing for a fortune 500 company. His was more a story of pulling himself up by the bootstraps. He didn't have the pedigree of Lisa, but he'd sacrificed and worked to get to this point in his life. He now wanted to settle down with a house, kids, and family. Lisa seemed like the one to make that happen. She was comfortable in almost any setting, country, city, boardroom or the basketball court. She loved warm weather and became a bit of a snowbird, going south in the winter months to avoid the brutal cold of the mid-Atlantic. She was very interested in William and how he had made it to the ripe age of 45 with neither chick nor child. It seemed his focus was entirely on upward mobility. She learned from her research that he was raised in NYC and had family down south that he would visit during the summer while growing up. He had climbed the corporate ladder without throwing much dirt on others and remaining humble in the process. That was refreshing and part of what drew her to him. He appreciated her love of travel and was a bit of road warrior himself, having driven across most of the US. He had over a hundred stamps in his passport, but it was their appreciation of music that bonded their relationship. There was always music in the background and many dates included concerts to see various jazz, neo-soul, and R&B performers. With both thinking of themselves as comedians, the comedy club was a regular as well. It was the music and laughter that keep the friendship light and easy. Both William and Lisa had demanding careers that required most of their time and mind. A year after meeting, the two were still going strong and had progressed from a friendship to a full-fledged relationship. The challenge was finding a balance between their busy work lives, friends and family events to make time for each other. They dragged each other to work and social events on a regular basis, all the while meeting friends and family, learning more about each other and strengthening the bond between the two. Lisa never let on about her secret profession and she knew the time was drawing near to shut down the business. She finally played with the idea of being a wife and mother. Interestingly enough, before William entered her life she had never considered the notion of marriage or family. Lisa loved her career and her freedom; she had her friends, family, and animals to keep her company. She never flung the doors open on her life, knowing it would take a special man—a champion—to handle her. Lisa was confident that she had found that in William.

She almost lost it all when work followed her home one night... To be continued in Volume 2, coming soon.

ABOUT THE AUTHOR

Sherrie is a science nerd and spa enthusiast, with her first book focusing on steps to open a spa. For her second writing adventure, Sherrie shifted focused and used the theme of love; with stories of her own and those observed over the years. When not writing, Sherrie is an educator and an avid traveler. Sherrie lives outside Washington, DC.